Tribune

50 cents

CTACULAR STUNS CITY

...day involved in a massive ...arch operation after a ...igh-profile cheese heists ...city.

... today asking themselves who ...hind the robberies, which have ... of the worst cheese shortages ...imes. Detectives said they are ...n open mind, but fingers are ...ted in the direction of notorious ...nal cheese thief "Fingers ..." McGraw has been at large since ...alentine's Day group escape from ...ays high-security prison.

...ice Department admit that they ...loss and the only option may be to ...Detective Jumbo Wayne Jr. out of ...ent to go up against the elusive ...Wayne Jr. was the detective who ...ht McGraw to justice over the ...ese Stilton" case, where an ...nely rare Hartington Stilton was ... and concealed for four months ...e a garden gnome. Such was the ...ic shock at the crime that McGraw ...sentenced to 18 years in prison.

Daily Tribune's ace reporter Louisa ...ne tracked down escaped convict ...nkie "Spatz da Rat" Capone to his ...wntown hideout for an exclusive ... on the unfolding recent events:

"Listen, dame, these ain't no nickle 'n' dime operations, see? This cat's real slick. In 'n' out quick, slippery like an eel. The law ain't got a chance!

Frankie "Spatz da Rat" Capone claims, "It's Fingers."

Lady, I'll give ya the scoop. We ain't talking no small-time hoodlum, this is the kingpin, Fingers McGraw! He's a real operator all right. He'll have made off with the loot and be aiming to stash it before the law catches up with 'im. I seen 'im nibble 'is way through two tons of gorgonzola in one night just to get rid of the evidence. If 'e is layin' low, there's a whole lotta mouseholes around town 'e could be hidin' out in."

Police are urging the public not to approach the mouse, who may be armed and dangerous, but instead to call their local police department immediately. Cheese shopkeepers have expressed their ... and asked officials for more ... on their premises.

6:00 A.M.: THERE'S AN UNEXPECTED VISITOR TO MOO O'SULLIVAN'S CHEESE PARLOR....

PETIT
LIVAROT

sniff
sniff

THE GETAWAY

Ed Vere

Margaret K. McElderry Books New York London Toronto Sydney

6:30 A.M.: IN AN ALLEY DOWNTOWN, THE SUN IS RISING ON THE LATEST IN A STRING OF SPECTACULAR ROBBERIES. MEET NOTORIOUS CHEESE THIEF FINGERS McGRAW.
psst!

FiNGERS iS ON THE RUN! BUT NOT FAR BEHiND
iS ACE LAWMAN DETECTiVE JUMBO WAYNE JR.,
IN HoT PURSUiT!

WANTED

Cheese thief
"Fingers McGraw"
wanted for questioning
in connection with
missing cheese.

If you have seen
the Mouse,
please inform
the Elephant.

Thank you.

11:00 A.M.: IT'S A RACE AGAINST TIME TO FIND A QUIET PLACE TO DISPOSE OF THE LOOT....
SCRAM, FINGERS!
MILK SHAKE
PHEW, she's hot! But I don't need company right now.

JUST iN THE NiCK oF TiME,
FiNGERS MAKES A SWiFT ESCAPE....

BUT WHO'S THIS?
COULD IT BE...

STOMP
STOMP STOMP

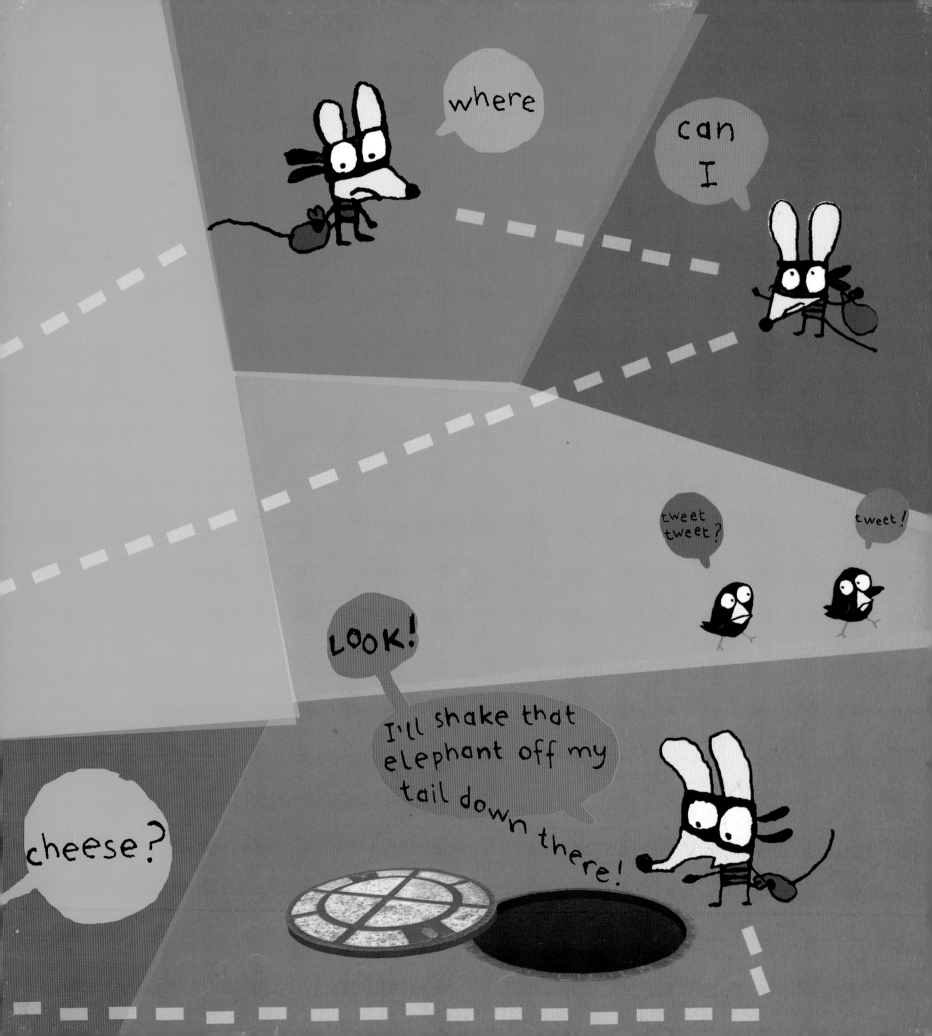

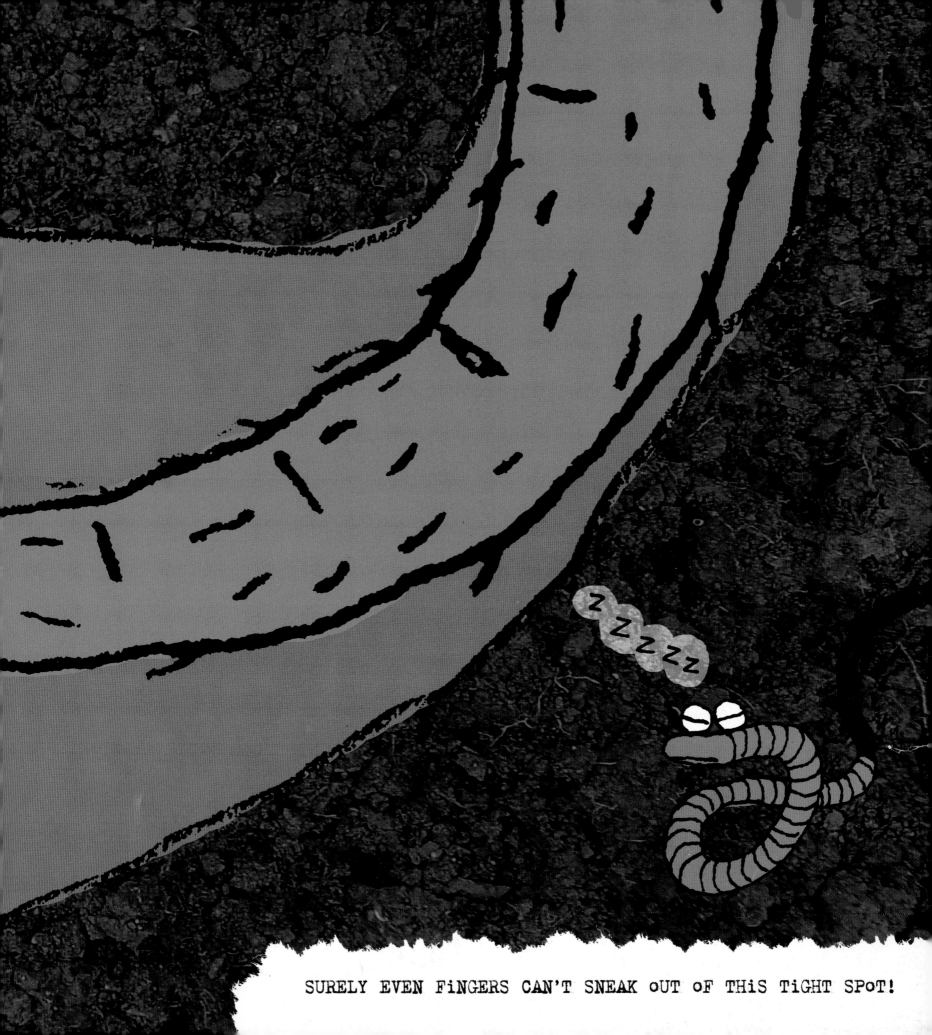

SURELY EVEN FiNGERS CAN'T SNEAK OUT OF THiS TiGHT SPOT!

IS THiS THE END FoR FiNGERS?...

11:00 P.M.: HIGH-SECURITY WING, MOUSEWAYS PRISON. AND SO WE LEAVE OUR WAYWARD FRIEND; AT LAST HE SEES THE ERROR OF HIS WAYS AND IS TRULY SORRY....

...OR iS HE?

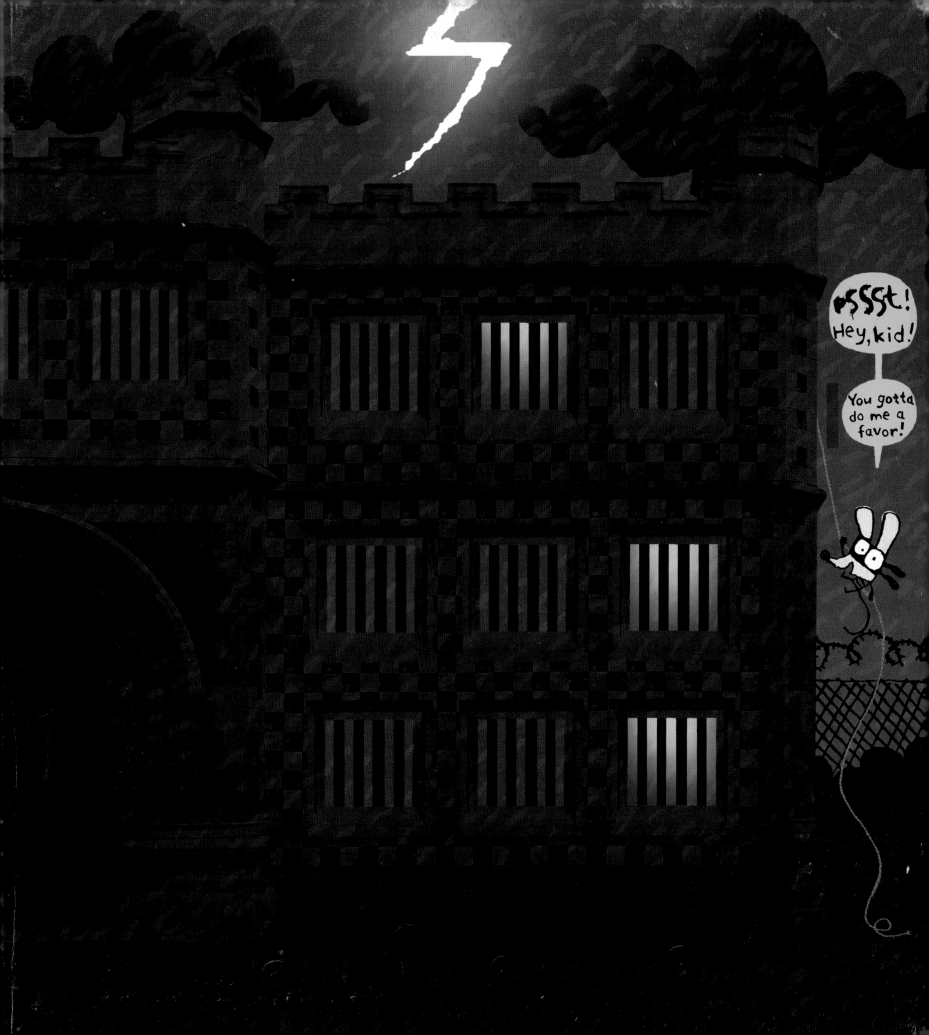

THE *GETAWAY*

McELDERRY BOOKS PRESENTS AN ED VERE PRODUCTION OF AN ED VERE FILM
"THE GETAWAY"
STARRING FINGERS AS "FINGERS McGRAW" BENICIO del RHINO jr. ROMAN RATANSKI
AND INTRODUCING JUMBO WAYNE jr. III AS "THE LAWMAKER"
FILMED ON LOCATION IN LONDON, BARCELONA, CHICAGO AND BILBAO
FILMED IN MOUSE-O-VISION WRITTEN AND DIRECTED BY ED VERE   www.edvere.com

Margaret K. McElderry Books
An imprint of Simon & Schuster Children's
Publishing Division
1230 Avenue of the Americas, New York,
New York 10020
Copyright © 2006 by Ed Vere
First published in Great Britain in 2006 by
Puffin Books, a publishing division of Penguin
Books Ltd
Published by arrangement with Penguin Books Ltd
First U.S. edition, 2007
All rights reserved, including the right of
reproduction in whole or in part in any form.
The text for this book is set in Vintage
Typewriter.
The illustrations are rendered in mixed media.
Manufactured in China
10 9 8 7 6 5 4 3 2 1
CIP data for this book is available from the
Library of Congress.
ISBN-13: 978-1-4169-4789-9
ISBN-10: 1-4169-4789-2

for Bicu

The Dai
DARING

The
The

In what is being hailed as one of the most spectacular escapes in recent memory, cheese thief Fingers McGraw has managed to evade security measures at one of the world's most highly defended prisons.

Police and the prison service were left red-faced last night after McGraw foiled high-level security systems and fled.

Only days before, McGraw had been captured in one of the largest mousehunts the city has seen in fifty years. McGraw led the police force on a week-long "goose chase," costing the security services an estimated $500,000 a day. As well, over half the police force were involved erecting road blocks and manning airports and seaports. Detective Jumbo Wayne Jr. had, at great expense, been coaxed out of retirement to go up against his old foe McGraw. The detective was seen as the last resort in what was increasingly becoming an embarrassment to the police department, as McGraw made off with over seventeen tons of designer cheeses from cheese-mongers throughout the city over a three-month period.

In what will certainly be seen as an attempt at damage limitation, the cops have set up an interstate checkp...
attempt to...

The *Tribune*'s ace reporter Louisa
again tracked down fellow esc
convict Frankie "Spatz da Rat" Ca
for an exclusive quote.

"Listen, dame,
like this, see. Fing
is a smallish mou
see and . . . er, we
see, I'm a rat and
lot of cons is lik
other creatures, y
know, like dogs
cats, sometimes horses. The point is that
these other cons is all, like, bigger
than what a mouse is, so a mouse being
smaller an' that can generally squeeze
out through the bars in the prison. It's
complicated an' that to explain, but . . .
er, well, the bars are, like, too big…well,
not exactly too big, it's the spaces
between the bars. They is . . . er . . . like,
too far apart. The mouse, see, 'e got the
knack of squeezin' out between the bars,
which is too far apart, see?"

This shock revelation that the bars on the
prison windows are too far apart will
almost certainly lead to a far-reaching
report into prison security methods and
practice. Bar spacing has long been a
matter for concern among the state
prison community but is se
costly to "

Fingers

captured
the city h
had led th
'goose ch
services an
as well over
involved er
manning air
Jumbo Wayne
been coaxed o
up against his
Detective was s